P9-CRS-537

Clatter Bash!

Gracias to Joe Lucas who, on his deathbed,
inspired the birth of this book.

—R. C. K.

Ω
Published by
PEACHTREE PUBLISHERS
1700 Chattahoochee Avenue
Atlanta, Georgia 30318-2112
www.peachtree-online.com

ISBN 1-56145-322-6

Cut-paper montage Illustrations created with various papers, watercolor and acrylic paints, pens, and markers. Text typeset in Gills Sans and Bart Thin Heavy; titles created with Bart Thin Heavy and Gill Sans.

Printed in China
10 9 8 7 6 5 4 3 2

Library of Congress Cataloging-in-Publication Data

Keep, Richard Cleminson.
Clatter bash! / written and illustrated by Richard Keep.-- 1st ed.
p. cm.
Summary: Rhyming text presents traditions used to celebrate the Day of the Dead.
ISBN 1-56145-322-6
[1. All Souls' Day--Fiction. 2. Stories in rhyme.] I. Title.

PZ8.3.K266Cl 2004
[E]--dc22

2004002201

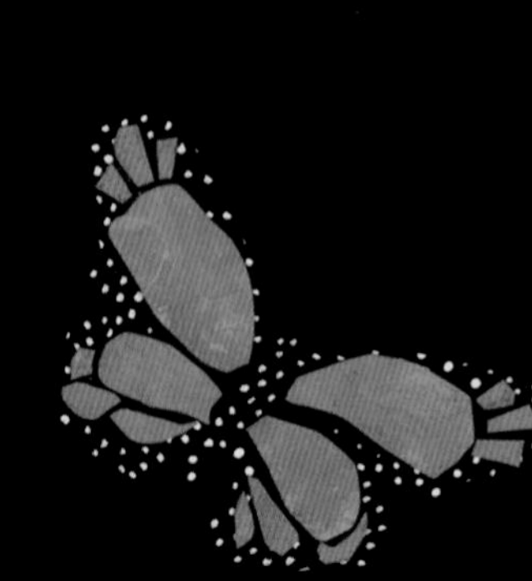

Clatter Bash!

A Day of the Dead Celebration

RICHARD KEEP

PEACHTREE
ATLANTA

Knock-knock! Shhh! Huh?

Rattle-rattle ¿Qué?

Creak-crack

Up we go!

Big *fiesta*! Yay!

Putt-putt Honk-whiz

¡Hola! ¡Hola! Hi!

Yak-yak Chitter-chat

¡Qué bonito!

My!

Flitter-flutter Butterfly!

Ooooh! Wow! Whee!

¡Buenas noches! Storytime!

Shiver-jitter Gee!

Sip-gulp Chomp-crunch

Slurp-burp

Yum!

La-la Sing-along Doo-bee-doo-bee-dum!

Whoosh-sploosh (oops!) Giggle-gurgle Splash!

Swirl-twirl Cha-cha-cha

Boom! Clatter Bash!

Sweep-sweep

Tidy up

Shush-hush...

Sigh…

¡Gracias!

¡Gracias!

Wink-blink   Yawn...   Snore...

¡Adiós! Good-bye!

El Día de los Muertos
The Day of the Dead

¿Qué? (What?) *Sí, los muertos.* (Yes, the dead.)

EL DÍA DE LOS MUERTOS is a Mexican holiday celebrating death. It is a day of both noisy fun and quiet respect.

In late October, towns and villages everywhere in Mexico—and many places in the United States—get ready for the big *fiesta* (celebration). Children dressed as *angelitos* (angels), *diablos* (devils), and *calacas* (skeletons) shout *"¡Hola!"* (Hello!) as they parade through town with their parents. There is music, singing and dancing, and the sparkle and bang of fireworks in the streets.

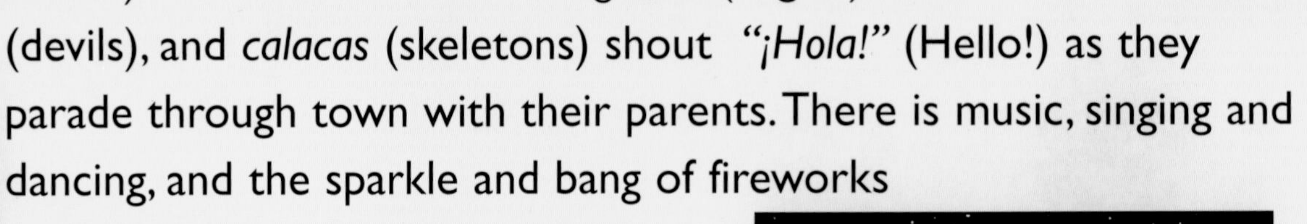

In the markets, there are bunches of orange marigolds—flowers of the dead. *¡Qué bonito!* (How pretty!) There are bins full of fresh *frutas* (fruits), *verduras* (vegetables), *quesos* (cheeses), and *hierbas* (herbs) for cooking special Day of the Dead feasts. There are chocolate skulls and tiny sugar coffins for sale.

There are masks and toys made to poke fun at death. There is sweet bread called *pan de muertos* (bread of the dead) baked with shapes of little bones on top.

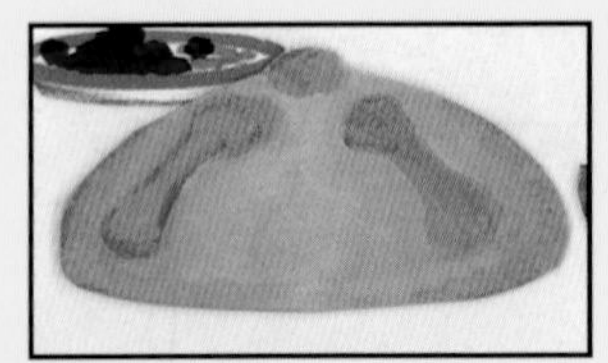

For dinner, people cook beans and rice, and meat or chicken with *mole*—a sauce made with chili peppers and chocolate. A corn drink called *atole* is served with the feast.

Ofrendas are home altars covered with offerings. They are made to honor beloved friends and family members who have died. They are decorated with candles, festive foods, toys, photographs, and *papel picado*—cut tissue-paper pictures—of skeletons at play.

On one of the nights, usually November first or second, it is believed that the spirits of the dead come back for a visit. Everywhere families say "*¡Buenas noches!*" (Good evening!) as they walk to the town cemeteries. They clean and decorate the *tumbas* (graves). They bring blankets to sit on and baskets of treats for a family reunion picnic. They pray for their ancestors to return, *por favor* (please). When darkness comes, *velas* (candles) flicker on the graves, lighting the way for the returning spirits. The smoky smell of *copal* (tropical resin) incense mixed with the scent of marigolds fills the air. Some people stay all night in the cemetery, playing soft music and sharing family stories. Most people return to their homes so the spirits can enjoy their own *fiesta* and say "*¡Gracias!*" (Thank you!) for this special night—and "*Adiós*" (Good-bye) until next year.

El Día de los Muertos is not a time to feel sad or afraid of death. It is a time for *familias* (families) to come together, share memories of past loved ones, and celebrate the joy of being alive!

Fin